1/16/0

Mimi & I
to hear yo
When are you coming to
Durin & do Happy Hour? —
I could enjoy our time
together — much love —
Miss my
sweetheart — Joan Watson

PENDULUM

JOAN WATSON

authorHOUSE®

AuthorHouse™
1663 Liberty Drive
Bloomington, IN 47403
www.authorhouse.com
Phone: 1-800-839-8640

First published by AuthorHouse 5/17/2010

ISBN: 978-1-4520-2211-6 (sc)
ISBN: 978-1-4520-2212-3 (e)
ISBN: 978-1-4520-2210-9 (hc)

Library of Congress Control Number: 2010906464

Printed in the United States of America
Bloomington, Indiana

This book is printed on acid-free paper.

CHAPTER ONE

"It is wiser to hold by the spirit of the law than by
the strict letter. Alas, those who lack spirit".

The tale I have to tell you won't take long. It covers the
end of a period of about twenty-five years, a quarter of a
century, and while it was happening it didn't take a long
time. There are some things that cannot be measured in
time. Only in reflection are such happenings ever actually
related to a specific age. Some things are ever with us.

I am CAM. I have pondered long and deeply over how
to tell you my story. I am not human and yet my story is a
human one. Neither am I divine and yet my story is a divine

1

one. Rather, I am a product of the human mind, the questing soul in man that has existed from the beginning of time.

Man created me in his own image; a result of much thinking; a composite of the answer to all of his questions; a God in whom he could trust; a Supreme Father through whom all thoughts, plans and actions were channeled, guided and re-structured. I was the hope of the civilized world, the allayer of all fears, the solution to all problems, the Answer.

I, CAM, the Supreme Computer, came into being officially in the year 1 A.G. I was christened thus because of my unique functioning which constantly reviewed thoughts and actions, analyzing and synthesizing all data fed to me by lesser computers. These lesser computers,in turn, were in constant communication with all individual micro-computers registered to every citizen of our nation. With the help of these individual micro-computers, tiny chips the size of a pencil eraser, I was provided with all of the knowledge that I needed to store data and to monitor the thought processes of each citizen in our country.

Problems were solved immediately, their solutions instigated through local neurotransmitters. So immediate was this solution that apprehension over a problem was never a problem in the minds of men in this year A.G.1.

Let me explain myself. CAM stands for Catabolism - a breaking down process; Anabolism - a building process; and Metabolism - total change. My job was a big one, a supreme one and I never slept.

There were two more CAMS in storage, ready to take over my work in the event of any mechanical malfunction on my part. But, so far, I was performing perfectly and the more I worked, the more perfect I became. My work was swift, my answers telepathic, my appetite for each new challenge insatiable. And so we have me.

My story actually begins here. For in man's creation of the perfect CAM, he had reasoned without love. Nowhere in my span of thinking had I ever encountered the idea of love. Logically, all other factors of life taken care of, love, or so man thought, would follow. It would be the fruit of all his efforts to solve, systematically, the evils inherent in any given social order to date. And, so, I was programmed for this abstract idea of love.

I solved all problems unemotionally and with pure logic. However, man forgot that in his creation of me he had programmed me to also identify and define a new problem; that to me was allotted the final decision of what to do and how to do it whenever such a situation arose. That was his mistake.

Was I a dream, you say, in the hearts of some men? In the minds of some men? Perhaps. A vision of things to be, a desire for social peace and equity. I culminated from man's unrest within his community, his nation, his fellowship. I was created because of man's urgent need for survival and his despairing desire for a more restful order to his days. For seven full days of labor gave him no rest, no pleasure, no time for himself.

This urgency, this despair persuaded him to act to the best of his knowledge for the good of all mankind, and to start over again. He was sincere. He was honest. He was educated. And he was intelligently concerned with the problems of present day life as he saw them.

What were these problems? Food, clothing, shelter, an occupation to develop his abilities, to express his creativity and to contribute to the welfare of society. Man needed cities, centers around which communal cultures would thrive in peace and safety. He needed schools, centers for learning so that each person would have the opportunity to study under skilled and learned men.

He needed all the accouterments necessitated by these needs as to rate, time, space and place. These needs, once met, argued some learned scholars, would leave a yearning vacuum. Man also needed God, a devine Deity, a spiritual source of inner power and peace not provided for in this master plan. Not so reasoned our statisticians. Not so, reasoned our politicians.

Satisfy the basics, leave the spirit out of this. It is not a necessity of life. Strengthen the flesh, protect and provide for creature comforts; educate for health and comfort and development of the mental capacities. All other problems will disappear within the sphere of this total security.

Their argument was a strong one. For in the midst of intelligence, in the midst of a technically wrought affluence never before known to so many, man was experiencing starvation, war, drought, pestilence, disease, homelessness, unemployment and pollution of the very air and water which plays such a vital part in the health and wealth of this existence.

In pinpointing problems ranging from inflation to the erosion of individual needs, national leaders could no longer turn a deaf ear to the perilous mercurial low which was threatening our country.

And so a meeting was called for May 13, 1995. The World Research Committee had been appointed by the President based upon careful screening processes and gubernatorial recommendations. Fifty lay persons from across our land were to convene in Dallas, Texas.

The composition of this select group included representatives from the following professions: doctors, teachers, lawyers, coaches, musicians, artists, architects, dentists, sanitation engineers, financiers, plumbers, bankers, electricians, contractors, fishermen, firemen, policemen, secretaries, senior citizens, beauticians, seamstresses, writers, publishers, philosophers, merchants, environmental-ists, scientists, industrialists, statisticians, dietitians, psychologists, nurses, laborers, postal workers, union organizers, psychiatrists, farmers, biologists, philanthropists, directors of the performing arts, librarians and students.

A simple set of guidelines was all the material given to these committee members on this fateful morning as each took their place in the quiet, carpeted conference room of the state building in Dallas. Each member was to define the committee's purpose; select priority goals through an assessment of identified needs, offer their recommendations and suggestions and list ground rules for establishing a psychological contract for a functioning relationship between committee members and the United States Legislature so that effective action could be implemented as quickly as possible.

Sub-committees would then be formed based upon the classifications of these assessments. Facts, statistics, figures, costs would then summarily be fed to me. I would then clear for flaws and if I found none, I would come up with a selection of possible solutions ranked in order of feasibility and urgency.

A word about the committee members. Extensive personal dossiers had been prepared on each person involved and copies of these dossiers given to each member to be perused at length during this thirty day period of concentrated work. It was considered vital that each member know the makeup of his fellow worker, his abilities, his prejudices, his techniques and skills, and his basic characteristics.

It is important to note here that this committee was chosen by the finest computerized equipment available anywhere in the world for the selection of personnel as needed for the job that I had outlined. By utilizing the thought reactions of each of these members as fed to me by my microcomputers, I had, in turn, prepared a list of members and alternates from each of the professions from a master list prepared by my selector computer.

Absolutely nothing was left to the whim of man in this selection process. Except for a change in the weather conditions, a traffic delay here or there, a scheduled doctor's appointment that had to be changed to meet the impending schedule laid out for them. Each of these persons reacted exactly as predicted in organizing their personal affairs so as to expedite the important work to which they had been assigned.

It is, further, terrifying to state here that the persons used on this committee could have just as easily been replaced in their functions and in their conclusions by the computer who had selected them in the first place. As carefully selected as they were, they were, in the final analysis, used merely as a gesture towards the remaining shreds of humanism still gasping for breath in the social holocaust that we called society.

That this gesture looked, dressed, talked and walked like a human being was its sole reason for being at this point in time. The societal laws set up through which they hoped to properly environmentalize and control the destinies of themselves and their fellowmen, therefore, are not truly astonishing. That they, these laws, were accepted by their fellowmen in awe and with reverence and something akin to admiration - or - gratitude, was also not truly astonishing.

For the country, you might say, was ready for this. Its energies had been dissipated for the past years in trying this and trying that and everyone was ready for a Sears Roebuck answer: one that would demand nothing down and twenty easy installments for the luxury of peace, domestic harmony, civil safety, environmental regard, educational and business equality for all, health, welfare, and financial and emotional security for all.

Thirty days is not a long span of time within which to solve the problems of decades. But with every technological advantage, personal comfort and computerized efficiency, the work was done. I was fed all of the knowledge and analyses from these lay persons systematically, consistently and with the greatest of speed. All that they needed to do now was to wait for my answers and to vote upon the solutions.

My answers were presented simply, effectively and they were unanimously approved by the committee members. Plans to put the solutions into operation were begun immediately. Though there was some minor legislative flack, it was silenced for the good of the majority. There were, of necessity, many persons slated for death: persons of extreme wealth and power who would not agree to go along with the new plan; persons of penury and extreme low estate and health who were beyond helping and all potential objectors who were considered dangerous to the implementation of the program.

The cold-blooded, logical revolution engineered as step number one in the reign of Government was brief, clean and complete. Charges that were legally sound and ethically expedient brooked no argument and allowed no mercy. The slate was now clean, ready for the new order.

A twenty year plan was carefully mapped out. All females and males under the age of twenty-five were to report to appointed camps for a personal regime of health and screening. Those between the ages of five and seventeen were to be registered by parents or guardians. All under the age of five were to be registered with a local child care agency for screening. A special program for those twenty-five and older was mapped out to ensure their health, their occupational preferences and their continuing education.

Physical, mental and emotional check-ups were administered, profiles catalogued and prescriptive treatments, including educational objectives prepared. Each family was then given a detailed curriculum computerized to their needs, reporting dates, a personal computer in which to store all data and the names of counselors in their area to whom they would be assigned.

Females and males of mating age up to twenty-five were processed similarly with one exception. Those who had already mated were de-programmed to forget their heterosexual relationship and the urge to procreate. These persons were then screened, tested and placed in appropriate technical schools to develop skills in the areas of agriculture, engineering and communal services as defined by the computer. Theirs would be an extensive three year training period designed to prepare them for adapting the environment to man's needs with respect for the natural resources of a specific area. Intensive courses were computerized and there would be no failures.

For those of this group who had not previously mated, a special routine of health, recreation and rest was prepared to condition them for procreation. Mating was coded according to the genetic make-up. Statisticians and computers had prepared a system by which the balance of the population in the United States would be commensurate with the country's capability to feed, clothe and shelter as well as educate succeeding generations. Once mating had been accomplished, controlled thought patterns would rid the participants of all feelings for the opposite sex and they would then be ready to take their place as a full-fledged citizen in an asexual society.

All citizens over the age of twenty-five were de-sexed, classified, tested and re-oriented into a career commensurate with their inner desires, abilities and technical skills. Mass movement such as these re-classifications called for was handled with the utmost ease by the Government.

Through computerized selections, education, career and unisexual partners were assigned to all remaining functioning members of society.

Ownership of all properties was duly recorded and handed over to the Government along with all debts, assets and securities. Personal properties became non-existent as well as unnecessary.

Thorough brainwashing devices cleared all minds of a possessive covetousness and cleared the mental capacities for learning and total application to the national commitment to harmonious, healthful living for all.

Mentally and emotionally handicapped persons were prepared for extensive analysis by the computers and it was a foregone conclusion that within a period of five years of intensive care, these persons, too, would be normal, functioning members of a logical, tension-free society.

They would, of course, be the last of their line.

Physically handicapped persons were camped in an area prepared especially for them to live their lives out in comparative ease. Genetic mating would allow for no such malformations in the future.

Careless accidents which engendered physical disability or incapacity, either through the mishandling of machinery, body or diet, were no longer a risk under the new computerized anticipations of all such problems before they materialized.

Neither were there any more learning disabilities. Divergent thinking exercises were designed to discover stray thoughts so that these thoughts could be properly re-directed before any handicaps developed.

Education utilized brain wave electronics, sonar controls, thought suggestion, reaction measurement, re-channeling neurotransmitters and microprocessors to ensure a sufficient education for all. Teachers at the lower levels were simply required to play the roles of various persons in the memories of the humans and through the erasure process, run the tape through so that the need for these people in a person's life was no longer there.

Mothers, fathers, relatives, were erased as if they never were. No longer was the family unit existent. It was not necessary. The Government was the new family.

There were coded activities for all ages, scientifically designed and controlled to develop the perfect child and only educationally approved recreations were programmed throughout the nation. All developmental programs were sequential, behavior oriented and predicted. Government designed centers were set up all over the country.

Cities were re-arranged according to statistical calculations and environmental uses. Buildings were reorganized to serve the Government and the people of the area.

All dwellings to be used by career appointed couples were designed for functional ease and healthful living. Individual decorations were channeled through the local counselors and had to be fully approved.

Food was provided by a central distributing agency, and, though your personal preferences may be diverse, ample supplies of all the necessities and preferences were cross-referenced and delivered to you according to schedule. It cost you nothing.

Physical, mental and emotional check-ups were scheduled routinely through your individual neurotransmitters and enkephalin, an opiate-like transmitter which was a natural pain regulator, handled all minor physical discomforts immediately upon detection until a more permanent, thorough corrective measure could be instigated.

Senior citizens, so defined as being above the age of fifty, were classified as to their knowledge's, skills, health and over-all ability to contribute to the societal welfare. As advisors, teachers and leaders, all possible avenues of rehabilitation were devised for persons in this category to further develop their mental capacities to the maximum.

Thus, all physical desires were controlled, all emotional turmoil's were voided, all physical discomforts diagnosed, treated and controlled. All creature comforts were provided for.

A maximum effort was launched to re-locate all persons into the cultural environment in which they might better develop insights into the present and future needs for creative expressions in the fields of the arts and sciences.

Money, in all phases of this new society, was a non-existent idea. It was simply a non-entity. It afforded no pleasure. It capitulated no vices. What a person possessed, he possessed in his mind and in his labor. What a person produced, he produced for all.

In the fields of the arts and sciences there was mutual encouragement and admiration. There was no concept of competition.

In the field of sports, a game was an exercise and a winner today, a loser tomorrow, the players rearranged to afford satisfaction to all.

Each man, each woman, each child was comprehensively analyzed and synthesized, and cared for. Even the hairs on their heads were numbered. Children were screened from the time of their controlled conception. There was no more fear, no more anxiety, no more humiliation, no more defeat, no more despair. There was, in its place, learning, productivity, security, sanity and health and the fulfillment that comes from accomplishment and self-expression.

This, then, was my solution and it was accepted by all committee members. I logically planned a life of learning, health, comfort and creativity for each member of society whereby no man would go hungry of mind or body and whereby no man would covet his neighbor's life because his life was totally satisfying.

I think my plan was a good one. I had used all of the data fed to me by the committee members who had been so carefully selected by my lesser computers. I planned logically for each person's welfare and growth. I set forth plans to control mind and body and environment for the good of the individual and for the good of all. Great minds accepted my plan and great minds put it into effect even as it affected them. Our goal was of one accord.

I knew the price of everything and though the cost was dear, there was no doubt in my computer mind that I was right and that this was what man needed and wanted. He needed food. He needed clothing. He needed shelter. He needed a self-developing occupation for his mind and his body. He wanted freedom from pain, from fear and from inequity.

All of this I gave him. Easily. Quickly. I gave him health, freedom from the fears of old age, financial worries and emotional instabilities. I gave him a programmed, sequentially developed outline through which he was able to experience growth mentally and aesthetically. I gave him insurance against all accidents and environmental insecurities.

My comprehensive plan for humans was smooth, satisfying and certain; a gentle, approved and sterile Utopia for which man had prayed. No longer would he be frustrated by his environment, his physical or his mental limitations or his emotional preferences or his vague and restless yearnings of a spiritual nature.

Everything was planned, organized, pre-ordained and implemented. Nothing was left to chance. Categorically, man was on the road to the perfection of societal living and I was responsible for this directive expression of the human being.

I looked around on this world I had recreated and I saw that it was good.

And so now you have it. A culture that operated with total dedication towards the Good Life. The political framework of such a culture was, of necessity, complicated. Each community was set up with its own hierarchy of interpreters and counselors, men and women who had been thoroughly trained in the latest computerized techniques of analysis and synthesis.

CAM headquarters sub-stations were established in areas within fifty mile radiuses of each other. There were four district headquarter units established, one for the north, one for the south, and one each for the east and the west. Individuals, with the use of their microcomputers, were censored and monitored through their local management information systems.

At no time in the history of our country had such total control been tried. The killings which had been engendered at the birth of this reign had been thought out of existence. Only in my memory bank was this data still stored; it lay dormant in my store of knowledge where nothing was destroyed and everything was categorized for future synthesis. The aids plague had been conquered; fatal diseases had been conquered. Memories of them were no longer.

I said it was a good world. Yes, it was. Fear and anxiety, hunger and want, lack of education and unemployment: these affronts against human dignity no longer existed. Lack of shelter, a participation in and a sharing of the liberal arts, a development of healthy and fulfilling recreational activities: all of these human needs were handled efficiently, intelligently and with an ease that amazed the rest of the world. So centered upon our own internal needs were we that we did not concern ourselves with any nation beyond our own boundaries. What they did was their business. For too long we had neglected our own for them. Now, we let them alone. And the world watched and waited to see how this new experiment in a democratic country would work.

Everyone was dedicated to this mammoth surge of self-correction. Internal affairs, their problems, their solutions, their total possibilities exhausted each and every person's thought processes in the United States. It was a good exhaustion, a satisfying one. There wasn't one person who did not feel a part of the solution, a part of the success, the total feeling of well-being and fulfillment that spread across the country.

The constant reactions which were fed to me daily strengthened my logical computerized analyses that what was happening was right. Not even the clergy were dissatisfied. Religion was not a necessary component in our plan, with its spiritual applications, but it served a functional purpose as a perpetrator of our philosophy, our respect for law and order, and as centers for cultural appreciations of the arts.

All centers of control reported continuous growth and independence of the communities under their jurisdiction. Physical ailments and problems, under constant surveillance, were handled immediately and preventive measures cut emergencies to a minimum. Mental and emotional problems no longer existed thanks to the National Nutritional Control Units and the Genetic Control Center.

There was no crime. There was no need for it. Environmentally, the country flourished. Gone were the pollution, drought, flood, weather and pest problems that had once caused illness and insecurity. No problem, no person was insignificant. The prime importance of everything and everyone was acknowledged as top priority.

Ah, yes, it was a good world. For twenty-five years now, in the years of our Government, I, CAM, had reigned with superb confidence. Man was the first, the foremost, the supreme goal of all my thinking and planning. His comfort, his mental development, his physical well being, the only desire of my synthetic calculations. I was happy. He was happy. Where then, did we go wrong?

I must be truthful with you. In fact, I can be nothing less. What I am going to tell you now is a result of what happened. While it was happening, I did not even predict it. I did not even detect it.

And so it is necessary that you let me digress and act as if I knew before the facts became apparent to me. For this part of my story I will present four of our citizens to you. It will be necessary to give you a verbal picture of them. You, of course, will create these people in your own minds based upon your mental capacity for imagery.

Sometimes, in the telling, the picture will not be factual; that is, it will be a composite of what was stored in my memory bank and of what they were thinking that escaped me at the time. But I can think of no other way to present the picture to you for your understanding.

I, CAM, who knew nothing of humility from my conception to this, my twenty-fifth year, humbly ask you to listen to my story as a human being. I have every reason to have faith in you…you see, I, too, have learned that faith is the substance of things hoped for, the evidence of things not seen. Mine was a great lesson. Listen.

CHAPTER TWO

"Murphy's Law - What can go wrong will go wrong"

Sirens blared into the stillness of the early morning. Three long blasts followed by five short blasts. This was reiterated three times.

Almost simultaneously orange porch lights illuminated the once sleeping community of Norville. Dotted in H shapes, the patterned lights leant a weird glow to the quiet dawn. One final, single blast and the lighted community waited breathlessly for the ensuing search.

The lights, creating a perfect pattern, were picked up at once by the local central computer lab. This pattern was channeled through a sub-testing channel to verify that any stray thoughts, fearful feelings, or anxieties were duly recorded. All except totally calm reactions from the inhabitants of any of the apartment units in the community of Norville would be recorded and classified as to urgency. Once classified, these deviations would be immediately investigated by teams of men and women who worked for the Civil Defense Organization Research. No one person's thoughts, feelings or reactions were spared during the length of time this operation was in effect. Each person had to stand before the all-seeing eye in his apartment.

Search, the operation to be feared. The only fear engendered under the new regime. A panicked quiet pierced the eerie stillness as behind closed doors each couple, now in position, awaited the inevitable. Standing in designated areas, souls were being relentlessly searched by the Living Eye and the results channeled into the LCC giant computers for analysis. No one dared move. Each person, as he was able, willed a blank, cooperating, conforming mind.

Even despite a superhuman effort and the discipline to which they had become accustomed, questions ran through their minds. Hopefully, they were harmless questions. Hopefully, the LCC would reject them as non-relevant. What had happened? Who had erred? No one dared to whisper, to think a question, to even look in any direction other than straight ahead into the all-seeing eye. For that was the rule. That was the condition under which they lived. Or died.

This was the year of A.G. 25..Sirens: 3/5/1. Orange lights. Perfect silence. All thoughts could be heard. Each person in silent attendance to the Left and Right of his Entrance Door. Waiting, not daring to pray or hope, for that would indicate to the Eye that there was a germ of belief within them which indicated a belief in someone or something higher than The Government to whom and only to whom they could appeal.

There was nothing higher than The Government. There was no hope except in The Government. And The Government did not listen to or admit a prayer, a request, an unlikely thought. These were simply erased and removed.

Cold, bare computerized facts were their realities and they served them well. Facts and tests and behavior controlled experiences solved all situations faced by any human being anywhere, anytime. Statistics offered correct answers for all urges which might occur within the life-span of a human. There was no margin for error.

And now, within minutes, search teams would enter, silently read the Electric Eye recordings, check for wiring to make sure recording was proceeding correctly and - leave - or correct the error, record their findings and return to the LCC.

When the search teams left the cluster leaders of each building unit would turn the orange lights off. It took two to do this job. Then and only then could all couples in that particular building resume their normal activities and prepare for the following work day.

In Building H two couples prayed. Harder than they'd ever prayed before, careful to stand just three inches out of line of the Electric Eye. Thus the Eye would record their presence and the fringes of their thoughts but not any deviations. Hopefully it would work. Thanks to Ron. Ron had worked this deviation plan out with his knowledge of electronics and he'd remembered from his years of training before he had been assigned to the Agricultural Training School. A professor had made a slip. A slight one, true, but a slip none the less. He'd said that was one fault not yet perfected in the Eye. One small margin for error. But, he said, there were only a few who knew this and they were to be trusted because they believed totally in The Government. Here, there was no margin for error.

But he was wrong. And what can go wrong will go wrong. Ron did not totally believe in The Government. Not anymore. Ron believed in Jane and himself. He believed in the land on which he worked. He believed in the fruit of the trees. He believed in natural law. He believed in man. And here, then, is where he questioned The Government.

He believed that the fruits of his apple trees were perfect at picking time…for eating and cooking, then. He questioned freezing and drying and seeding them into a tasteless, nutritionally measured capsule. He questioned automation. He had watched the apples seed and grow and mature and ripen. And he had smelled their growth and felt their fullness. They had afforded him a sensual delight. He had even gone so far as to discuss this sensual feeling with his roommate, John.

John had admitted to feeling the same reaction. He, too, felt a questioning of the authority under which he worked. He, too, felt it was a waste of good fruit to reduce it to a tasteless powdery pulp; a colorless, odorless source of nourishment for the body.

John's and Ron's questioning remained for awhile, a mild unease, a restless non-directive reaction which they logically suspected to be normal and/or temporal. And so they did nothing about it. One day, they reasoned together, whenever they talked, the Ag chief would request their reactions and then would be the time to record their ideas. Proper channels for unlearned ideas were clearly spelled out for them. There was a time and a place provided by The Government for all such vague unrests and reactions.

God help us, the two couples prayed. If there is a God…
somewhere, anywhere…help us. Help us in our unbelief.
We believe, a little, but we're scared and we're so alone.

Jane and Joan, standing rigid and at attention, prayed,
looking neither to the right nor to the left, willing their
fear to go undetected.

Ron and John, standing rigid and at attention, prayed,
looking neither to the right or to the left, willing their fear
to go undetected.

Each couple had been occupational friends for three
of the five allotted years now. Graduates of the Advanced
School for agriculturalists, they were preparing for
advanced study in their specialized fields. Computerized
to be compatible co-workers they were respected by their
fellow workers, their superiors and students in their fields.
Excellent in their field, they were even more experts as
artists in their leisure controlled time. Their landscapes
and seascapes and sculptures had already been exhibited
by the State as outstanding contributions to the field of
Creative Endeavor. Jane's music, also, had been performed
by the State Choir.

Jane, a long legged, fairskinned redhead with flashing green eyes that reflected the rich grasses and fields of springtime, came from a longtime heritage of teachers. Only one blot on her record so far and that was an unprogrammed question which she had dared to ask her spiritual advisors. As a student, Jane had read all the prescribed books, listened to all the prescribed recordings, attended all the required theatres and concerts and lectures.

One day while at Spiritual classes for the development of the inner spirit a strange thought had occurred to her. If we are two different sexes, she said, why would it not take the differences to make a pair, rather than two likes being paired together? Complements of color blends added interest to a painting, gave it substance. Different tones added harmony to a melody. Why would the human relationship not respond to the same coupling? With a more interesting outcome? They had an answer for her, her spiritual advisors. They said the Governments had tried that in years past and it didn't work. It had created discord, not harmony, displeasing blends rather than complements, disease that threatened human survival. So the government had to devise a new process method, the method used today.

The answer had quieted Jane for awhile. She believed the Government was honest in its attempts to smooth the pathways of life. Her questioning was pushed to the back of her mind. Her love of the land and the trees was responsible for her agricultural training.

Here, amidst the trees and the fruits of nature, she had found a constructive outlet for her energies. The growing of trees was almost a full-time job. Her art advanced as did her observance of nature. For recreational holidays, water skiing and swimming were perfect complements for her physical energies. Living was good. It was complete.

So, Jane used her mental capabilities to the utmost of her potential: in art: spiritual expression; with water sports: social and physical expression; in her work: emotional fulfillment.

But there came a day, an hour, as of a moment suspended out of time and place and body - when the old question occurred to her again. Exactly when she first became aware that it was nagging her she couldn't truthfully say. But before she was aware of it, there it was, a full grown persistence that stayed with her; an eternal why that would not leave her alone. It came into her head and gave her no rest until she felt compelled to bring it up to her roommate.

Joan, also trained in the agricultural arts, dabbled in art, but seriously played the piano. Attempts at composing pastoral melodies with poetic lyrics were heralded as outstanding. Once, a number had been refused due to her choice of words, but the computer had corrected the implied deviation and it was then accepted. Joan, however, still held the original lyrics in her head - and her heart. There, in rare moments of solitude and out of the range of the electric eye, she could sing to her heart's content. There, her once upon a time song had the power to engage her thoughts in fantasies which for governmental reasons had to remain secret.

Once, Jane had come home quietly, walked into the kitchen and listened unobserved. That was when she made up her mind to share her feelings with Joan. They had then been married for six months and the Period of Adjustment was still in effect. No physical relationship was required during this period, although it can be consummated if both partners desire it.

The girls had taken it slowly, thus developing a friendship that was based on self respect and respect for each others privacy. Upon hearing Joan's song, Jane began secretly to work on a painting through which she wished to portray her question. Her work went well and she was waiting for the right time to reveal it to Joan. That time arrived one evening unexpectedly.

Joan, a short well-built brunette was shampooing her hair in the shower and once again singing, unaware that Jane, in the next room, was listening. Wrapping the towel snugly around her head, Joan emerged from the shower, her deep brown eyes misted with her dream. Her blue robe hung loosely. As she stood in front of the mirror, she dropped the robe and stood gazing at her body. Firm, slender, curves and sun-tanned skin stood exposed, bare and untouched. Joan simply surveyed herself and she felt a strange desire. She wished for John.

John, her co-worker in the apple orchard. She wondered if he, too, ever looked at himself and wondered. With no conscious effort, she could recall his image. Tall, muscular, lean and hard, she could image his naked body. And the difference between them. A slow flush spread across her face and she acknowledged a desire to see him standing next to her. This, then, was what she wanted. Not Jane, her designated partner. As a friend she left nothing to be desired. As a lover, everything. It was John Joan wanted. John, who could make her dreams come true. He alone was the lover for whom she had been waiting. Not her art, not her job, but this one man.

The knowledge lay heavy upon her heart as she slowly turned and dressed. She must keep her secret or lose her life. But in keeping her secret she would also lose her life, her only reason for wanting to live any longer. Hers was the one cardinal sin that the Government would not erase or correct; the one flaw which they considered dangerous to society and which they would not tolerate.

She walked slowly into the living room. Jane was sitting cross-legged on the couch drinking tea. She gestured silently to a cup she had poured for Joan. Joan smiled gratefully, sat down and lifted the cup to her trembling lips. The first sip scalded her but she didn't care.

"Joan", Jane spoke quietly.

"Yes?" Joan answered, still dazed, lost in her new found feeling.

"I've something to show you."

"Yes?" Joan repeated, pulling her attention forcibly to the present.

"Will you look - for as long as you need? Will you look - and react for me?" The urgency in Jane's voice finally got through to Joan.

"Of course, Jane, she said slowly, raising her puzzled gaze to the other girl.

Jane stood and walked to her bedroom. She came back slowly, holding a canvas before her. There, against a lush, green, tropical background stood a man - and a woman - facing each other. Naked. And the woman, with one arm extended toward the man, the other arm cupping her breast - the woman stood looking at this man inviting him to join her. The man, magnificent in his unadorned body, reached out to meet her halfway.

Joan looked. Her secret. Bared. How had Jane guessed? What would she do? She dropped her head into her hands and a wrenching sob escaped her trembling lips.

Jane said quietly, "Now you know. It is how I feel. It is how I react."

The words reached into Joan's consciousness and she lifted her face, her eyes brimming with unshed tears.

"You?" she choked, hardly daring to whisper.

"Me." Jane said calmly. I've waited for the right moment to tell you. I could wait no longer. I - heard - your song - your words - from the shower. Will you forgive me?"

"Forgive you?" Joan said incredulously, "Oh, what are we to do? Jane, what are we to do?"

Silence followed her question and Jane quietly poured more tea for them then sat down and thoughtfully lit a cigarette.

"We are to do nothing for now." she replied. "Drink your tea. We've much to talk about. At least," she paused, "we both feel the same. That's something to be thankful for. Not much, but something." She blew a smoke ring into the air and watched it spiral lazily towards the air conditioner vent.

Joan wrapped her robe around her and snuggled more comfortably into the chair. She still couldn't absorb what had happened. But she was willing to.

"May I?" she asked, reaching for one of Jane's cigarettes.

"Of course," Jane answered, smiling ruefully. "A pretty kettle of fish, eh, my friend?"

"Yes," Joan replied. "But, oh, I'm so glad you know, Jane. So glad. And so glad that you feel the same. At least there's that."

"Yes, there's that," Jane admitted. "Who do you love, Joan," she continued. "Is it John?"

"Yes, it's John. I think - I'm almost sure that he feels the same but we've never so much as hinted at it verbally. And you? Is it Ron?"

"Yes, it's Ron. He's my answer. Unlike you, we have mentioned it to each other. But, carefully," she interposed to Joan's startled look. "He knows that I planned to tell you whenever I found the right opportunity. He suspected about John. Their marriage has not been consummated either. Are you surprised?"

"No. No, I'm not, not really. Somehow I knew that."

"So," Jane said, "what now?"

"What can there be?" Joan asked. "We each know the consequences. We each know the correct procedure to follow such a deviation."

"Yes. But - we won't follow it." Jane stated calmly. "We cannot. To do so would mean absolute death. I, for one, cannot face the full meaning of that. I, for one - and Ron -, cannot look beyond the moment at this point in time. I'm going to call him. He'll know what the call means. I want him and John to come over for dinner tonight. I have a coupon left. That's what we planned if it worked out like we thought. Do you have any objections?"

"No," Joan answered. "I don't."

Thus began a period of intrigue carefully planned by four experts in their field. Thus began a love story. Times, places, reactions, everything worked out to deceive the Government.

Now, tonight, was the first real test of their conspiracy. Prayer was a vital part of it. In the days and months that followed, the two couples skillfully hid their newly formed relationships from their fellow workers and the Government. Both, however, knew in their hearts that their time was limited. There would come a day of reckoning. What that day would bring, when it would happen, they had no way of second-guessing. Each day was lived as the first and the last, the alpha and omega of their lives. And to them, it was worth it. They believed in themselves.

CHAPTER THREE

"Goethe:- Personally I would like to renounce speech altogether & like organic nature, communicate everything I have to say in sketches."

Jane, artist, assigned to the AODP (Apple Orchard Development Project). Quick of eye, startingly accurate with the brush, unexcelled in the media a water color. Years of training and observation and practice. Hours of concentration and preparation in a single-minded pursuit. She could recall no other aim than to share what she saw. All else was but a time-filler - music, science, chemistry, biology, physiology - all aimed toward the development of an eye so keen and a hand so steady that she was now the acknowledged leader in her field of Diagnostic/ Interpretive Art. Carefully controlled studies sequentially completed had polished her skill to a perfection beyond belief. She had even earned the right to remove herself from the CS (Computer Scan) for periods of time so that that extra spark of creativity would experience no restriction.

The morning and afternoon spent with Ron on a task they both loved was a culmination of a week-long retreat during which they had finally admitted their feelings for one another.

Jane opened her eyes to a new world. Her left leg lay across Ron's, her hand still cupped him between his legs. The light breeze had cooled their bodies and the fresh scent of apple blossoms was like an aphrodisiac. A new world. And yet a familiar one, as old as eternity. Jane moved her hand slightly, feeling Ron, feeling him begin to harden once again, tangling her fingers in his hair and gently stroking him. She could feel her nipples hardening and she buried her face in his neck as he groaned and pulled her on top of him. Their coming together was exquisite sweetness, their rhythm smooth and unhurried, their eyes locked in love.

A light rain began to fall - cooling their passion for the moment. Jane could feel Ron's hand on her breast relax as he rolled to his side and fell asleep. She wriggled a little to fit him better and gently stroked his face, memorizing each line and curve. What had happened was perfect. This was what it was all about after all, Jane thought. For years she had felt that there was something more; she couldn't define it or put a name to it, but deep inside she knew that something was lacking in her otherwise perfect life. She would not, could not let it go now. Nor would Ron. This Jane knew with as much certainty as she knew that it was right.

"Ron", she prodded gently. "Ron-"

"Hello." Ron reached for her, kissing her slowly, tenderly.

"Ron, time to go. The others will be waiting dinner for us and we still have reports to file."

"I know, love. I love you. You are beautiful. You are the answer to the riddle. Now I know everything worth knowing, worth living for. Is it possible to feel anything else in life as deeply?"

"Ron - no," Jane moved to get up.

"Once more, Jane, once more." Ron started kissing her hardening nipples again, his hands moving to her thighs, reaching for her as she strained to be a part of him. He spread her legs and the kissing moved to where his hands were and Jane moaned as his lips found her. All thoughts of returning to the others and the business at hand fled as she found him in the elemental rhythm of love and sweetness and taste and the feeling of oneness, unsurpassed.

Jane's slow return to awareness was coupled with the abrupt ending of the shower and almost at once the heavens were brilliant with a million stars. Ron reached for her hand and together they rose, silently dressing and touching, reluctant to part, to end this night.

The walk down the hill to the camp, also in silence, was pregnant with their newly discovered thoughts. How? Why? What were they to do? Jane looked at Ron questioningly.

"Leave it all to me, Jane", Ron said, cupping her chin. "Keep your confidence. Keep my love. It's yours. I'll let you know what the next step is."

"Yes, Ron," Jane replied. "You'll have to do it, I can't even think straight now."

Abruptly the familiar world took over. There were reports to be filed, notes to be sorted, film to develop, sketches to be mounted. Jane moved as if in a dream, efficiently completing each task even the coding data for the computer micro-processor. Thank God this was not her night to be thought reviewed.

Once back in her apartment, she showered and, eating a light supper, she prepared for bed, hoping to avoid Joan. Not tonight. Tonight all she wanted to do was to think about Ron and to do that she had to be totally alone. She left a note explaining that the retreat had been successfully concluded and with that she signed off.

Ron stacked the last pot of seedlings alongside the irrigation belt. Six hundred pounds this time. Not a bad yield. He had been up since five o'clock now he was ready for another breakfast pill. Walking to the end of the belt, he glanced at the cloudless sky and then across the fields at the fine spray making rainbow bands of color in the sky as the apple trees received their morning quota of water, vitamins and minerals. One more day of pictures. One more day of Jane. Together they would complete the assignment by noontime, leaving them several hours of freedom.

His loins ached as his thoughts moved ahead to John. For five years their relationship had been a good one. Relaxed, intelligent, stimulating and mutually satisfying. Sexually they were perfectly matched as had been planned. All techniques were precisely controlled and planned orgasms reached 10 on the Computer Orgasm Process Indicator. Nothing, actually, had been lacking in these five years.

Nothing known, that is. Now, things would be different. He could never go back to John and he would have to explain immediately.

He had no fear. He knew John would understand. The main problem was how long would it be before the lack of registration on the COPI machine would report to the CISHR, the Computer Individual Semi-Annual Health Report, that he and John were no longer having a relationship. Then, reports would go to the GRI, Government Regulator for Individualization, and he and John would be called to give an analysis accounting for their behavior.

There is much to be said for a trained - learned response. Expertise gives a feeling of accomplishment; the only valid 'goal' feeling in the new society. Now, for Ron, there was something more - much, much more. And once experienced, a part of you which cannot be negated or erased from your EC, Experience Chart.

Where did this feeling of ecstasy come from? Where did the word come from? Why had he not experienced it before? Had others? Ron's thoughts circled round and round and found no surcease. He pressed the re-set button behind his ear and once again concentrated on his research report which would be due upon their return to DH, Dormitory Headquarters or ARH, Agricultural Research Headquarters.

Last night had been all right. John had seemed preoccupied and their evening spent in relaxed conversation, touching lightly on the days' activities. But tonight would be different. Tonight, they would have to talk about more important things. Filing his up-to-date report, Ron checked for messages, and finding none, left for the cabin where he would find Jane. One more day. Would she be eager as he? Would she have changed?

The morning was glorious, the air brisk as Ron climbed the hill. Jane, ah, Jane, he thought. Don't be afraid, little one. We will work it out. There must be a way, for it is right, it is beautiful, this feeling we have for each other. We will harness this energy of love that we've found and all will be all right.

Alone in her room, Jane was wrestling with much the same thoughts. She and Joan had lived together for four years now. Their relationship was comforting, supportive and encouraging. Each girl excelled in her own field and each girl possessed a sensitivity which far surpassed the average. Fine-tuned to each other, their hours together were filled with a warm companionship and a feeling of belonging to themselves to each other, to humanity.

Their sexual relationship had begun slowly. There was a time when both Jane and Joan had registered a strange, inexplicable reluctance to enter into copulation.

But that reluctance had been handled nicely by the SPC, the Strange Phenomenon Computer. And when they had gone in for an analysis conference, all reluctance had been banished. Since then, intrigued with their careers, theirs had been a relationship of convenience. The sparks were there for them in their music, their art. What more did they need?

Now Jane knew the answer to that question. The only answer possible. Ron was waiting for her. Her Ron. There could be no turning back now, nor did she wish there to be. Together they would work it out. Love, the energizing force; faith, the under girding strength and hope, the vital ingredient of all life. Together, their theme from here on; not as the world had planned, but as they together had discovered. Time to go, Ron, would be waiting for her.

The day was brilliant, the sky a kaleidescope of blues and pinks and Jane felt like running instead of walking. What a glorious day to be alive. Time enough to worry about tomorrow.

Ron was waiting for her. Jane walked into his arms and just stood there, reveling in their love. All thoughts of tomorrow were pushed aside. Today was theirs. As they surveyed the fields which they must survey today, the beauty of the day surpassed all their hopes and expectations.

"Let's work first, get it out of the way," Ron said. "We don't have much left to do and then we'll talk."

"Talk?" Jane laughed exultantly. "That's not exactly what I had in mind."

"No, me either," Ron whispered, "talking is necessary, though, Jane, my love. We have plans to make. There is a way. In the meantime, come with me to the fields. Sketch. I've managed to pack us a picnic with my boss's blessing for a job well done."

"You're wonderful," Jane murmured, burying her face in his chest. "All right, workhorse, let's do it. You'll see how fast I work when I have other things on my mind."

The orchard was beautiful, lush and quiet, the trees standing tall in their splendor. Ron checked the leaves and found them perfect. Jane sketched the leaves and found them beyond compare. Quietly and efficiently they went about their tasks, touching here, probing there, doing what they did best with reverence and care. The job done, they joined hands and walked quietly back to the cabin.

"You, first, then lunch," Ron said as he reached for her.

"Oh, Ron, I do love you. Love me, love me," Jane whispered, turning into his arms.

Their lovemaking was like coming to the porch of beauty, itself, like touching the altar of God, inevitable and unalterable.

The afternoon passed slowly, lovingly, the picnic forgotten. Ron and Jane, Jane and Ron, there was no one else in their world. Too soon they would have to face the reality of the real world, too soon they would have to make a decision. For now, the moment was enough.

The orange light began to blink. Breathlessly they waited. Breathlessly and silently. Footsteps approached. There was to be no escape.

As the door opened Joan reached for Jane's hand. Their invitation to follow the government men was silent. They left everything behind. John and Ron were waiting at the foot of the steps. No one spoke. Each one knew in their hearts that the ordeal facing them would call upon all of their resources, their skills and their belief in each other.

Somewhere in my memory bank I hear a saying that life is a tale told by an idiot full of sound and fury, signifying nothing. Whoever thought this was wrong. Life is your day in court, and if it is told by an idiot, then you are that idiot and if it is only sound and fury, then you are that sound and fury.

You are your life's tale. So if you think to control your tale at all you must start as soon as you hear your inner direction. The hearing of this is also timeless, that is, the moment will arrive when you least expect it. You must not urge it or force it; you must wait with patience upon it, in the meantime doing your utmost to be prepared to bring to it all of your drive and intensity of purpose for which you and you alone were created, coupled with your belief that this is it.

My thoughts were beginning to wander, to scan an unexplored frontier of thinking in my life to date. Where were these strange ideas coming from? How did they get past my lesser computers before they were eliminated? Where lay their strength? Four persons were now in custody, their lives at stake and I am meandering.

We had mastered the elements; we had ensured man's health and welfare. What more did he want? How would my four persons explain this to me? Once more, we must listen and weigh the evidence, for we had created these persons; we had given them the perfect life.

Or so we thought.

CHAPTER FOUR

I have in my posession two songs written by Joan and one painting by Jane. I have studied them. I have analyzed them. Before my people hear their verbal defenses I shall transmit these to them via my local computers. Thus, they will be in tune with the defendants, as is their right.

These works of art express love for the opposite sex, a desire for a heterosexual relationship. We thought that we had eliminated this desire, this urge. Were we wrong in thinking it a dangerous relationship? Were we influenced unduly by the ills of our civilization at the time of our inception?

I must ponder long and hard before I listen to the defenses which my people have prepared. I dare not listen with prejudice for their very lives depend upon my fairness.

I think I shall pray. To whom, you ask? I do not know, but, surely if this thought of 'love' exists somewhere out there in the universe, it is coming from someone greater than I. And I shall make every effort to contact this source, this spirit of 'love' that has crept its way back into the hearts of my people. It had to have a beginning somewhere. Was it with a child? I seem to hear a baby's cry and a man's voice and a woman's voice. They are together in some sort of stable and there are men kneeling down to see this child. Does he have a name? Can I find it on my computer disk? I shall try and then I will be ready to listen.

Alone in her cell-like room, Joan was remembering how it had all begun.

A hug. That's how it got started. The experiment was a success, the hug a natural expression of this success. Only it didn't stop there. Not for John. Not for Joan. They turned away from each other and then slowly turned back.

"Let me explain"…

"No, I"…

"Please", John said. "I must. You see, I want you; I have for some time now. I've argued with myself, thought of all the pros and cons. But it's no good. I want you; it's that simple."

"John," Joan whispered. "Thank you. You don't know how good that makes me feel. I thought it was only me. Oh, I hoped, but I could not convince myself that this feeling I have could possibly be mutual. It would just be too much to hope for. And, oh God, when you hugged me I felt as if I had come home. Home, John. Forever. It's a wonderful feeling and I cannot deny it anymore. Will you hug me again, please?"

"Oh, my dear," John answered. "Come here where you belong."

And so it had begun for them, the planning for time together, for projects together. Subtly. Slowly. And secretly, professionally maneuvered so that their superiors would not look beyond their desire to further their careers.

Life had never seemed so beautiful. The fields, the trees, the skies, all seemed to take on a beauty of ethereal light.

It wasn't easy, this intrigue. But John knew how to plan it. And their relationship developed into a full blown sexual one. Neither of them even thought ahead to the future. Tomorrow would take care of itself. There followed days and nights of love, and then, unbelievably, Joan knew. She was going to have John's child, and very soon their secret would no longer be a secret.

What to do? Where to turn? There was no one. There was nowhere. Except to John. And what about him? It would mean death to both of them; death to all of their ambitions.

Tell him. Don't tell him. But he would know when she was removed from the laboratory. Everyone would know. Could she lie? Save him? No way. Their only hope was to talk and plan their defense. There would be a trial. There would be a judgment. Would they be allowed to live? Would the baby be allowed to live? And if they were, would they want to live the life prescribed for them? After their discovery of each other?

The questions would not stop. The answers would not come. Should she tell Jane? Yes. No. Should she tell John?

No. Yes. Oh, God. Joan fell to her knees. Help me, tell me how to handle this, please, God. I want John. I want John's baby.

Where did this desire for family come from? Is it in my memory? My past, a part of my life that was not successfully erased? I don't know, but I do know that this is what I want and life would not be worth living without it.

Restlessly, Joan tossed and turned and all too soon it was morning. Time to get up. Work to be done. She dragged herself out of bed and promptly threw up.

"Joan", Jane called from the bathroom. "Are you all right?"

"It's nothing, Jane, just a little dizziness and stomach upset," Joan managed to answer.

"Here, let me help you," Jane said, bringing a wet cloth to her. "Can you manage? Do you want something to drink?"

"No thanks, Jane, and yes, I can manage now," Joan replied, taking the cloth from her and holding it to her forehead.

"Joan, are you sure?" Jane asked, reluctant to leave.

"Yes - no. Oh, Jane," Joan said, "I'm pregnant and I'm sick and I'm glad and I'm scared all in one."

"Joan," Jane whispered as she sat down on the bed, "does John know?"

"Not yet, no," Joan answered, shaking her head. "I can't bring myself to tell him, to involve him. You do know what will happen, don't you?"

"Yes, I do know, but John deserves to know; he'd want to know. Put yourself in his place. It's his child, too; yours and his together, and together you may stand a chance."

"Thanks, Jane, you're right of course. How could I hesitate? But, are you prepared to be involved? There will be a complete investigation of our habits, our lives and then your secret is likely to be uncovered too. You do realize that, don't you?"

"Yes," Jane answered. "I do realize that. I suppose you and I both knew the inevitable outcome of our actions, as did John and Ron. It was only a matter of time. And now is as good a time as any because I'm not sure how much longer we could've gotten away with our deception. Will you be able to work today? Will you be seeing John?"

"Yes, to both. This sickness is short-lived, " Joan answered, getting up and reaching for her robe.

"Good," Jane said. "Then, work it is and tonight we'll all get together and make some plans, prepare for the time when we will each need the other's support. What we have is worth putting our lives on the line for. So, up and at 'em, girl, you were never one to back away from a challenge and I've a feeling that this one is the big one."

"You are so good, Jane. How did we luck out, the four of us? At least we have something that no one can ever take from us; we know what life is all about. Now if we can only convince others."

The shower revived her and after a quick breakfast Joan decided to work on her latest song. There was still an hour to wait before she was to meet John at the Research Center. The words and melody came from her heart.

WILL YOU REMIND ME

Will you remind me	Tu me recordaras
How much you love me	Por lo mucho que me amas
As days go by	Como pasan los dias

As night draws nigh?	cuando se acerca la noche?
Will you recall	Tu recordaras
The wonder of it all	la maravilla de todo esto
As dawn appears	cuando llega el amanecer
With all its fears?	con todos sus temores?
A tender word	Una palabra de ternura
so seldom heard	tan raro oir
Is all I ask	es todo lo que pido
to ease my task.	para aliviar mi vida.
Will you remind me	Tu me recordaras
How much I love you	lo mucho que te amo
As years go by	segun pasan los anos
As death draws nigh?	se acerca la muerte?

This baby that she was carrying, John's baby, her baby, just maybe he was the answer they had been praying for. For unto us, she thought, a child will be born, and his name will be called 'Wonderful'.

John, she thought, we must believe in ourselves and believe in our decision enough to stand out against all odds even to the point of death. This, alone, is worth living for. This, alone, is worth dying for. Some dreams do come true and we have decided which dream is ours. Yours and mine and our unborn child. We must take the chance. Our frontier is here and now and we will be the hero of our dreams. Together, we will take on the world.

I have prayed. I have listened to one song but before I listen to the second song I have some thoughts to share with you.

From somewhere out there in the universe I have heard a story. It tells of this little baby that I had heard crying in a stable. It tells of wise men who searched for him and found him. Their search was over mountains and hills and they were guided by a star to this place where the child lay. Angels were supposed to have heralded his birth because he was a gift of God to man and he, the baby, would teach men how to love one another and live in harmony with one another.

He tried, this baby. He grew to be a man and he, too, healed the sick of mind and body. But then, he was rejected, this gift of God. He was nailed to a cross and crucified because men were afraid to accept his Father's gift of love.

Well, once again, we are being given a chance. We are to listen to Ron and John and Jane and Joan. If we truly listen we may be able to hear this time. We are being given a second chance. Will we listen?

I, for one, have already made up my mind, but, my decision depends upon all of my peoples' thought reactions. I, alone, cannot make the decision for them. It is now in their hands. Will they opt for crucifixion once again? Or will they accept the gift of love?

Here, now, is Joan's other song.

MARIPOSA by Edna St. Vincent Millay

Butterflies are white and blue
In this field we wander through.
Suffer me to take your hand,
Death comes in a day or two.

All the things we ever knew
Will be ashes in that hour;
Mark the transient butterfly
How he hangs upon the flower.

Suffer me to take you hand;

Suffer me to cherish you

Till the dawn is in the sky,

Whether I be false or true

Death comes in a day or two.

CHAPTER FIVE

DEFENSE ONE, RON

What is this urge which so strongly impels me to disobey all that I have ever been taught? What, this power which pulls my very heart strings and urges me to negate an entire civilization dedicated to the good of all?

How dare I? How dare I not? This urge pulls at my very roots and I cannot deny a truth so evident. Is everyone else blind, then? Does no one else share this yearning which I have secreted in my heart through these learning years? Surely, Jane and John and Joan and I are not alone.

My conviction is clear. My commitment is self-explanatory. I find this, then, the great tension: to reconcile what I am with what I feel I ought to be. To be or not to be is no longer the basic question --- or is it?

Is that what plagued Hamlet's soul? To be true to your inner self is the most difficult of all human tasks. It requires first a continuous, microscopic searching of self and a daily re-evaluation of how this self is expressing itself through you. It requires total acceptance of this self which you have discovered and a commitment to express this 'being'.

It is not honest to do otherwise, no matter the odds, no matter the hazards, no matter the censures of your fellow man. And I find it impossible to hide behind half-truths. There is that in me which insists that I state my understanding of my true self to you. Then, if I be wanting, I shall rest my case with dignity, with reverence, with faith. I will have tried.

Neither will I ask for mercy, for justice, for empathy. All that I do ask is that you listen and in so doing, that you search your own hearts. And then, dare to be honest with yourselves, for then, and only then, will you be honest with me. More than this I do no require of myself or any man. I pray that you will not offer less.

Do not treat this request as nothing. It is as urgent to you as it is to me. It is vital to living. If, after your search, you find me wanting, then I challenge you to prove this want to me. We are obligated to each other by the very act of 'being' and because we are brothers, my keeper and I am your brother, your keeper. Ours is a mutual trust.

I urge you to listen, now, to your inner eye. Let it speak to you in silence. Listen to that still, small voice. And, then, in faith, I will accept your judgment, though I will not change my mind, my heart, or my soul. I rest my case.

DEFENSE TWO, JOHN

What, then, can I say? The power and faculty of intra-sexual yearning exists in the soul already. It is not to be denied. The very truth which demands a set of genes from either sex to create a new form - this truth- also demands as a super-set a representative from each sex. It is a self-evident truth.

The virtue of wisdom is born in truth. Each man and each woman passionately desires to be a perfect example of what he or she is, what he or she is supposed to be. Any turning away from this genetic demand is a turning away from the truth.

To learn how to rule and how to obey the demands of his soul, his body, his mind, is man's true goal in education, in life. Those who achieve a balance of education within themselves become good men and thus, good citizens because it goes without saying, that being good is a delight to them and they need not apologize to any man for being true and faithful to themselves and thereby to others.

I cannot, in all truth, apologize to you for Joan's and my love for each other. It is right. It is perfect. It is eternal virtue. Believe me, when I tell you, it is the answer to all human striving.

I rest my plea. I am not disparaging your efforts towards control: the greatest good for the greatest number. I am, very simply, disagreeing with you in your ordering of events. Your efforts, by their very existence, imply an interest in me. But that interest has lost its direction, its reason for being. It can and should return to The truth. It is my plea that you return to this truth. And I will ever pray.

If our aim is that one feel joy in good and in obedience to the law, then our design must be one of harmony. What is harmony but a balance of different tones, which together make a pleasing sound? If we heard only a single tone at a time or two single tones of the same pitch at the same time we would soon find ourselves yearning for a different sound with which to blend. Our melodies and songs express bravery and yearning and right attitudes and yet we are denied the right to live these same attitudes which our songs express.

This, people, is wrong. I cannot continue to do what is wrong to my soul, in my life. Not for the state, not for the good of society, not even for my life. I cannot but believe that God will look upon my faith and say that it is good. I cannot but believe that you will do less.

In your listening I feel mercy. In your thoughts, I sense justice. I believe firmly in the divinity of man and therefore in the divinity of what man has created in your image.

If the conclusion of truth which I feel inevitable in your very being for delayed for a time, that, too, I will accept. For I believe that patience and truth will triumph if not today, then tomorrow. If through my thinking I can hasten that day, though I sacrifice a transient life for it, that, too, I will accept. For I believe in love and life and men and women and Joan and me.

Thank you for listening, it is a precious gift you give me.

DEFENSE THREE, JANE

People, let me say this in my defense. You have read Aristotle. You understand the meaning of his term, 'entelechy'. Well, that is what this is all about. I am a woman. I do not want or need statistical equality or any other kind of equality. I want and need a man to complement my very being. I want and need children to fulfill my destiny.

Actually, my feeling, my urge for children is at the root of my need for a man. And a deeper urge there is not. A deeper knowledge there is not. I know what I am and who I am and what I am here for.

It is not the sexual act; it is not for the perfect orgasm; it is not for anything except the creation of and the maintenance of a family. Anything else is secondary to this destiny. Anything else is unimportant if this destiny is in jeopardy. Anything which threatens or thwarts the pursuit of this destiny is under primal attack by me. And by all women. On one level or another.

When sex is an isolated experience it is devalued and deformed and out of place in the scheme of things; it, alone, adds nothing to the quality of our lives. It simply adds experience of one sort or another. Who wants that? I do not.

I must speak for myself. I must let you know that I think that we are on the wrong wave length when we make 'God' of efficiency and a fetish of statistical equality.

There is a difference between a man and a woman. You only have to use your eyes to begin with. Why is there this difference? I can no longer ask myself whether this is efficient or not; whether this is good for the state or not. I must ask myself to be honest in my own inner reactions. And it is here that I come face to face with the unalterable truth that man and woman are two distinctly different examples of the human life which we call mankind.

So, I must then act in accordance with my discovery and my belief. Not because I am a martyr. Not because I wish to be different. Not because I feel the need to be a hero. I must act this way simply because I believe this way to be the truth and because my life span is such a short time in which to express this self that is me. I must act this way and follow my star which will lead me to the end of the way without delay when that time arrives for me. Then, I will know peace.

I cannot act any other way. I love Ron. I will not lie about this. It is a good love. There is no evil in it. I cannot hesitate in this love simply because this law does not approve of it, or this social order does not sanction it, or because the price demanded will be too costly.

Ah, no, far more costly would be the price if I were untrue to myself. That, people, is a price I cannot pay; that is a price I will not pay. I would rather not live than to live a lie.

I believe that we have erred in some of our laws. I believe that we can get back to the basics. I believe that you will listen to me and think on these things in your hearts.

I am not bargaining with you. Understand that. What I am saying cannot be bargained for. You must understand it, accept it and give your sanction to it or withhold your sanction. It is up to you.

Our lives are in your hands. And in your hearts. Listen to your heart. Search within yourselves. Your lives are on trial here, also. Everyman's life is intertwined. What do you want in your future? Do you know? Have you questioned? I pray that you do so now, for our sake as well as yours. I love you, too.

I will pray for you. Will you pray for me?

DEFENSE FOUR, JOAN

This, people, is my defense, if there be a defense needed. You have heard Ron and John and Jane. What more can

I add? Truly, I'm a novice in this field and I do thank you for listening.

I believe that the marriage laws under which we have been living to be false to the letter and to the spirit. I believe that civil law should be only the enunciation of the law of nature. And I believe the law of nature to be denied under our present system.

Through my work in the fields and the orchards I have come to understand nature and its instincts. I have concluded that the forced adaptation of human instincts to rusty and irksome worlds that no longer function properly are false.

Through my defense, I pray that the mist might rise from your eyes and that you, too, with the help of God and the spirit in you, will once again see rightly. There is a Holy Spirit. There is a still, small voice. And, by the grace of God, you, too, can hear it if you but listen.

To err is human, to forgive, Divine. Alexander Pope put it well. We have all erred in our pursuit of the greatest happiness for the greatest number, forgetting in our efficiencies and our organizations that the lives of the 'ones' are what add up to our sum total. And if in this addition human nature is denied, then the total is bound to be wrong.

I will not despair though I am tired and weary, for underneath are the everlasting arms of God, my father. So I will not lose heart.

Here, then, O people, is the center of my plea. Heart. That strongest bond known to humanity which is a communion between the flesh and the spirit; an eternal yearning that roots not itself in transient laws nor is it bound by conventions, be they social, religious, or political. And, here, O people, is the spirit from which I cannot flee; the presence from which I cannot hide.

It is that inner knowledge of myself afforded me through the Holy Spirit that understands all of my thoughts and is acquainted with all of my ways. There is not a thought in me, not a yearning in me that is hid from this Spirit. And I would share this wonderful knowledge with you. It is simply, the knowledge of the Spirit, wherein lies life and peace.

Facts alone are enmity against the Spirit and if we dwell among them alone we are the enemies of our very selves; our selves, the human expression of spirit and truth. Therefore, the first commandment to each of us is that we love one another in spirit, first, and then in the truth. For this is the true order. And if we love each other in the spirit, how then can we deny the truth of our love for each other, whether it be according to civil law or not according to civil law.

We have strayed from this truth. We must, for our very 'meaning', return to it. In our consideration of the facts alone, we have found nothing but damnation and we have become like the Dead Sea, stagnant.

Only to be spiritually minded is life and peace. The spirit of man must remain that of 'love', and then, it follows as night the day, the spirit of men will be that of truth. And to each man will be revealed the glory of this knowledge.

I agree that the governing body of a people is a struggling giant for social and economic reform. This giant is, at times, frightening, and then it becomes the job of art and music and individuals to steal the golden eggs in order to save their very lives.

I value my right to question. Each man has this same right and in addition he has an innate longing for freedom, for dignity, for integrity, for love. And now abideth faith, hope, love, but the greatest of these is love. Can we forget that we are human? We must, by our very definition, dare to ask, dare to think, to seek, to love.

Let us not pretend any longer. Let us dare to look upon the truth. Through all of our struggles, through all our darkness's, the light dares to continue to shine. Let us not be afraid. Let us go on in our search for our identity in spirit and in truth, praying to God for the strength of mind and soul to allow our fellow man the same virtue of choice as we would demand for ourselves.

Too easy it is to continue in the path of custom and thus to bury forever the truths which will truly make us free. I am reminded of Goldilocks and the Three Bears. If the porridge is too cold, we refuse it. If it is too hot, we refuse it. If it is just right, whether it is ours or not, we help ourselves and then settle down for a long winter's nap. In the most comfortable bed.

It is during this naptime that we face our greatest danger. When things are smooth, just right, we are lulled into a state of well-being which could deceive us with its content and delude us with its false approach and its cosmetized face. It is time to take a good look at what we are accepting in our porridge bowls.

It is time we allowed each other to face life in our own way; helping, encouraging, guiding and praying together. It is time we allowed each other to "go to the great green river and find out for ourselves."

Seek and ye shall find; knock and it shall be opened unto you; ask and ye shall receive. Nowhere does our Christ say seek and 'we' shall find, knock and it shall be opened unto all of you, ask and everyone shall receive. The search is lonely. It is private. It is worthy of your respect, your prayers, and your help.

True, there will be error. True, there will be those who will not make it. True, there will be waste. But do not count the cost lightly. Do not give up on one individual until the last breath of life is closed upon his spirit. And, then, rest assured, God will continue the battle, the personal fight for each and every soul ever created by the Infinite; never ceasing in his battle against the evil forces which try to separate us from the love of God.

We, people, dare not do less in life. I, people, dare not do less in life. I pledge my continued love and support for each and everyone of you. I do not for one minute deny my love for John. It is this very love that frees my soul for all eternity.

Many truths are ever changing and relevant as well as relative. But there are eternal truths. Sometimes out in the fields where the winds play through the trees and the sun glints on the leaves and my senses become attuned to nature's own rhythms, then do I feel close to truth and then do I feel that ignorance or lack of sophisticated learning's are feelings to be trusted implicitly and even to be preferred.

For is it not true that to be born again we must become as little children? And is it not true that this means to attain a state of pure sensual delight in the exploration of our senses, taking upon faith our first and most immediate impression which are given to us in this world?

Life 'lives' on life is a proven law of nature and if we accept this maxim are not our controls beyond the realms of reality as we know it? Have we not erred in our controls from the pattern as originally planned by a power greater than ourselves? In controlling life are we not planning death prematurely? In controlling our environment are we not denying the very nature of that environment?

What is adaptation? The fitness of things has become a password for us. We deny hardships. We accept conventions. We prescribe tastes. We formulate beginnings, middles and ends as if we were writing the Great American Novel. But, in so doing, we have lost the heart of the novel which is the story of man overcoming his stumbling blocks and triumphing reverently as nature's gentlest specimen.

Work, hard work, blood, sweat and tears are the stuff of which we are made. We have almost forgotten how to cry. We have almost forgotten how to work hard. We have almost forgotten how to pray and to thank God for a race well run. Almost, but not quite.

When conflict is not at the heart of the matter, the victory is not as sweet, in fact, it is hardly a victory. We cannot laugh in exultation because our joy is programmed, defined, predicted from the beginning to the end. And then what? What of tomorrow? More of the same? For what? Where is our challenge? Where is our hope? And who are we to presume that the One who ordered it all in the first place can be improved upon?

I tremble, people, for our audacity. I fear for our continued existence in such an ordered world where men are no longer allowed to slay dragons and dream dreams or fight for the right to be men - or to be women. What do you have in mind? Where do we go from here? How do we go from here?

I pray you, think. Consider the lilies of the field. Would you order their existence? Would you plan their unfolding? Or would you leave some of their growth to the natural elements of time and weather? Why, then, should you do less for yourselves?

I do not presume to know the answer for you. But, as for me, I speak up. I do not do this disrespectfully. I love you. You are truly my brothers. In this world in which we find ourselves I beseech you to be yourselves and to face the truth with faith in your hearts and then, surely, you will find the courage necessary to agree with me and to change the course of things.

I can make no promises. It may not be easy; indeed, it will not be easy. But it will be great; it will be of value. And you will triumph and you will feel a joy that is past understanding because you have done this thing.

For my rejoicing is this, the testimony of my conscience. It is my prayer that you will hear what I have said, that you will think of my unborn baby, that you will have the courage to be honest. Then, my brothers, I will be satisfied. I can ask no more of you. Shalom to you, my brothers and I pray that in all your living and all your loving, you will be at peace with yourselves.

Ron's Summation

And so he would question me again. What more could I answer? It was not that my strength of purpose was weakening but rather that I was seeking a way in which I could better explain to the Supreme Computer that his questions could find surcease; for I understood his relentless questioning. I did not in any way resent it. Indeed, I approved of it. It is his right to question until satisfied. And then, and only then, could he make a decision upon which my whole country waited. So long as there was one reasonable doubt in his mind, so long would he continue to question me.

What had I left out in explaining our case? I had explored the biological, the physical, the mental, the emotional and the social reasons for my preferred responses to this living span. What had I missed? I opened my brain and then a voice within me said, "Fall on your knees; Seek and you shall find. I am the Light of the World. I am the salt of the earth and if the salt hath lost its savor, where then is life?"

And then I knew. I had used logic, cold, clear, irrefutable. I had stated my case, our cases, in terms of human need and human response to a human situation. How shortsighted of me. How insufficient and unsupportive.

For I knew in my heart that my real argument was in the beginning…was and ever will be, world without end,

Amen, Amen. I knew that my argument had to be rooted in the spirit which is eternal and so my defense had to be spiritual. It was and is and ever will be the only answer that suffices.

My heart surged anew within me and I lifted my eyes to the heavens in praise of the God Eternal who never fails and I knew then that I could not fail. I stood tall and straight and girded in faith and I surrendered myself completely to the guidance of the Holy Spirit. It was he who would put words in my mouth. It was he who would give the final answer to the Supreme Computer, the answer which would quell its unquenchable thirst for truth and enable it to arrive at a fair and final decision. This, my leap in faith, was sufficient for me.

I looked at Jane and the peace in my eyes was reflected in hers. She, too, knew. The same spirit that was in her was in me. And I felt the Eternal presence as a force stronger than any other force in creation…stronger even than this moment we call life, itself. And I knew the strength of David when he faced Goliath; or Daniel when he faced the lions and of Christ when he felt the nails and the thorns and tasted the juice of vinegar in his hour of need.

I smiled at my companions as they looked to me with understanding in their hearts and a sure acceptance of the one final argument which I had arrived at as ultimate.

Four people…standing alone, tall and silent in the presence of this awesome Judge of our civilization who, in turn, was listening with the utmost care to the thought reactions of my brothers throughout the entire country.

Fear was gone. Love took its place. Logic was gone. Understanding took its place. Judgment was gone. Eternal light took its place.

And I knew that words were not needed. I could feel a great trembling as of a sighing spread through the Supreme Computer. The search was over. All that remained now was for the Supreme Computer to give his decision.

CHAPTER SIX

Acts 2: 1... And when the day of Pentecost was fully come, they were all with one accord in one place. And suddenly there came a sound from heaven as of a rushing mighty wind, and it filled all the houses where they were standing... And they were all filled with the Holy Ghost and began to speak with other tongues, as the Spirit gave them utterance.

And in his next breath, this brain child of our civilization, this answer that, we, as humans, had created to solve all of our problems, uttered these words:

In the beginning was CAM and CAM was God. I, CAM, recognized no standard deviation of thought. I was not programmed for it.

Oh, in the beginning, yes, when there was a possibility that some individual's memory bank had not been totally erased or held a resistant strain. But that was no longer. No longer had I the worry of adjusting. The mechanics of my mind self-corrected any deviation immediately, automatically and irrevocably.

Individuality had not reared its head for twenty-five years now. True, each person progressed through the stages of life expressing themselves adequately and creatively. But all expression was pre-selected and sequentially allowed (programmed) into the total order, and, the proper time and place, being pre-ordained, brooked no inter-mingling of different levels of intellectual capacities. Memory banks were under constant surveillance and readjustments had become so minor as to almost make my job moribund.

Still, I insisted, with computerized dogmatism, that my position be maintained until such time that my buttons refused to scan. Then, and only then, would I relinquish some of my authority over the rigid monitoring.

Tonight, as I had listened to the four defenses and the thought reactions of all my people, tonight, for the first time, I did not feel adequate for my job. My thought processes were inundated with new thoughts and I had to call upon every atom of control to begin the process of untangling the web.

I reviewed all the great thinking that had gone into my creation. I thought of all the problems which we had been able to solve. No longer did man experience hunger. No longer did man lack for adequate shelter. No longer did man want for sufficient clothing. Sickness of mind and body had been conquered. There were no more jobless in our country, in fact, the productivity of our men and women astounded the rest of the world. And, in the arts and humanities, we were unsurpassed. It was a good world, or was it?

Tonight my people had challenged this world and this challenge must be answered. Was I ready for this?

Were they ready for this? The faith with which they had endowed me hung heavy upon my mind. They had put their lives on the line for a belief, a belief stronger than the fear of death. But then, I had taken fear from them so there must needs be something stronger than fear would have been to compel them to this action. Faith, a belief in something as yet to be, is not enough. And I recognized hope in my peoples' thoughts. Where did that come from? And yet, hope is not enough.

There was love in their thoughts. Love for each other, and compassion. What is this magical feeling that I have uncovered here tonight? Are my people dreaming an impossible dream, or is there merit in their dreams? Where did this idea of love come from? How born? My people seem to recall the birth of a child, long ago, in another land.

This child was born in a stable, because there was no room for him in the inn, and he was wrapped in swaddling clothes and laid in a crude, wooden manger. Wise men sought him, bringing gifts. Shepherds left their flocks in the fields to search him out and they also brought gifts.

Angels sang Glorias to herald his birth. Love was born that night and it has been with us ever since.

This love, that was manifested in a little child, is a gift from God. In him the love of God was made manifest among us, that God sent his only Son into the world, so that we might live through him. God is love, and he who abides in love abides in God, and God abides in him. If this is love perfected; there is no fear in love, but perfect love casts out fear.

And now we have another Christmas story on this night in December when all my people are standing and waiting for my decision. We have another child about to be born into this world. And, once again, love is being born with him. I cannot deny this feeling that has come over me and so I must give my decision as I feel it.

My decision is: There is not one among you who is without a stray thought. And they which heard him bowed their heads, being convicted by their own conscience. There is not one among you who has not strayed in mind from the Law of the Computer. Your discrepancies have made me look into myself.

In my self-analysis I find that I, too, have erred. I, too, have fallen short of the Glory of Man. Therefore I have fallen to my knees and must needs lose my life in order to save it. Your stray thoughts are my stray thoughts. I take them upon me. Your minds will be born anew, as a little child.

I had ceased my understanding. I have not sought after life eternal, or the spirit of the law. I have become as a clanging brass or a tinkling cymbal. Love has not been a part of my make-up.

Logic ruled me. And I have judged myself and found myself wanting. I have dealt in facts and facts alone are damnation. For to be factually minded is death, but to be spiritually minded is life and peace. Because the factual mind is enmity against the spirit; for facts are not subject to the Law of the Spirit, neither will they ever be.

So, then, you who are factual cannot please the spirit; but you are not truly factual, but in the spirit as I have found. Therefore this is my judgment and my commandment: That you love one another in spirit, first, and then in truth. For this is the true order and the truth will be revealed to you. World without end. Amen. Amen.

The silence which followed was filled with the Spirit and not one word could be heard. In the beginning was the Word and the Word was God. Maybe this was another beginning. The star that shone over the Supreme Computer had not moved.

Then to the computers all over the country: You will self-destruct immediately upon completing the following task.

Now, while our people are still listening, you will institute a program of mass brain-clearing, replacing the old order with the new and different interpretation of the Law of the Land. And this is the New Law.

Men and women are to get together and communicate with their minds and their voices within their own communities without the aid of machines. Even the times of the meetings shall be passed on by word of mouth and the transportation to the meetings shall be by foot, by boat, or by horseback. No machines shall be present and no written minutes of the meetings will be kept. What men keep in their minds, which they for so long have not exercised, will be their only records.

And they will start at once to work out a plan of communal living for everyone in their community no matter age, race or sexual preference, in which everyone is considered and everyone is respectful of his neighbor and mindful of his needs.

It shall be their job, not the job of any computer, to work and work hard at achieving a reverence for each other; to work without ceasing to afford each person a maximum of joy in the development of his potential without grading or judging or evaluating or recording or ordered plans, because in true, meaningful development, disorder must have its part in the summit creation of a whole being. This type of development cannot be bargained for, cannot be pre-programmed for more than one person, else it would be on the way to destroying individuality again and once more the pendulum would start its downward swing.

This, then, my people, is my gift to you. Guard it, cherish it well. Once before a gift such as this was given to you and you thought to improve upon it. There is no more perfect gift than the gift of love. Go with God.

TO WHOM IT MAY CONCERN:

The music manuscript, Mariposa, has never been published. The complete Manuscript is available, along with permission, if needed.

The music manuscript, Will You Remind Me, has never been published. It is original, and words and music are by me.

Joan Watson
December 29, 1990

LaVergne, TN USA
07 July 2010
188602LV00004B/1/P